ADVENTURES OF
LITTLE CRITTER®

BY MERCER MAYER

Sandy Creek

Sandy Creek
387 Park Avenue South
New York, NY 10016

ISBN -13: 978-1-4351-2647-3
Manufactured in China.
Manufactured 09/2011
Lot 11 12 13 14 15 SCP 10 9 8 7 6 5 4 3

TO THE RESCUE!

BY MERCER MAYER

For Zeb, our rescuer!

Dad goes to the basement.

He has work to do.

I am working, too.

I am working with my tools.

I am tired of working.

I hear my dad walking
up the basement stairs.

8

He calls me.

He needs my help.

The door is stuck.

I will help.

I twist and turn the doorknob.
I can't open the door.

I say, "I will get keys.
Keys will open the door.
They are hanging in the hall."

I climb up and get them.

There are many keys.

I try them all. Oops!
One breaks off.

"Don't worry, Dad," I say.

"I will call 9-1-1.

14

Stay there.

I'll be right back."

I dial 9-1-1 on the telephone.
A very nice 9-1-1 lady
answers the phone.

I say, "My dad is locked
in the basement
and can't get out."

The 9-1-1 lady asks me
my telephone number.
I tell her.

She asks what my address is.

I know my address, too.

I tell her.

I tell Dad that help
is on the way.
Suddenly, I am hungry.

I go to the kitchen.

I make a snack to eat

until help arrives.

Soon I hear sirens.

First the police car comes.

Then the fire truck comes.

I see Fireman Joe.

"We have to get my dad out of the basement. Follow me," I tell everyone.

I will show them
where to go.

Fireman Joe tells Dad
to stand back.

Fireman Joe takes a big ax.

He breaks down the door.

Hooray! Dad is safe!

Everyone helps take the
broken door outside.

The policemen say good-bye.

The firemen say good-bye.

"Thank you
and good-bye!" I say.

Dad says I am a hero.

I just called 9-1-1.

JUST A
LITTLE SICK

BY MERCER MAYER

To Diane, Bonnie, and Rita,
the elves

I am just a little sick today.
Mom says, "No school.
You need to stay in bed."

Being just a little sick
is fun.

I get breakfast in bed. Yay!

It is just plain toast. Yuck!

"I want Fruity Nut Crunch,"
I say.

Mom says, "You are too sick.
Go back to bed."

"I am not too sick
to play video games."

"Yes, you are," says Mom.
"Now go to bed and rest."

I am not too sick
to fly to the moon
on my rocket ship.

"The rocket ship ran out
of gas," Mom says.
"It needs to rest."

I am not too sick
to build a tent on my bed.
I am hiding from my bear.

Suddenly I don't feel good.

My bear and I go to find Mom.

Mom sends me back to bed.
She takes my temperature.

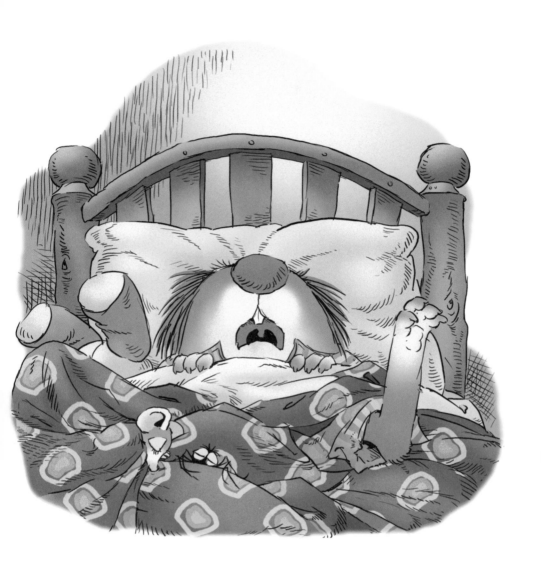

"You have a fever," says Mom.

I say, "I am sleepy."

I wake up from my nap.
I feel great!

I get dressed.

I will go out to play.

Mom says, "Oh, good,
you are all dressed.
Let's go to the doctor."

"But I am not sick anymore,"
I say.

Mom takes me to the doctor
anyway.

We wait and wait.

I put on a funny-looking robe.
The back is open.

The doctor checks my throat,
my nose, and my ears.

The doctor gives Mom something
to make me feel better.

We go home.
I can't wait to go out
and play with my friends.

"Oh, no," says Mom.
"The doctor said
you have to rest all day."

I am tired of resting!
I ask, "Can I please go
to school tomorrow?"

I changed my mind.
Being just a little sick
is no fun.

GOING TO THE
FIREHOUSE

BY MERCER MAYER

*To Arden and Benjamin,
our two new high school graduates!*

Today my class is going
to the firehouse!
I dress like a fireman.
Time to fight a fire!

This is Fireman Joe.

This is his dog, Sparky.

Sparky is a fire dog.

Fireman Joe has boots.

He has a jacket.

He has a helmet.

I have boots.

I have a jacket.

I do not have a helmet.

Joe slides down the pole.
Sparky howls.
That is what he does
when there is a fire.

We see a fire truck.

It is big.

It is red.

It has hoses and a ladder.

Joe checks the hoses.

He lets me help.

Whoosh goes the water.
This hose is working fine.

Joe checks the ladder.

He goes up and up.

He is in the sky.

Hello, Fireman Joe!

Joe checks the siren.

It goes Ooo! Eee! Ooo!

The siren is very loud.

I cover my ears.

Joe tells us about fires.

He tells us smoke goes up.

When smoke goes up,
we must go down to the floor.

I get on the floor.

Joe tells us what to do if we
are on fire.

Stop,

drop,

and roll!

I stop, drop, and roll!

Fireman Joe smiles.

He has a surprise.

He reaches into his truck.

Helmets for everyone!

I put on my helmet.

Joe tells me I will be
a good fireman one day.

Ding! Ding! goes the fire alarm.
I wave good-bye to Fireman Joe.
I wave good-bye to Sparky.
Time to fight a fire!

Fireman Joe is ready to go!
Sparky is, too.

THIS IS MY TOWN

BY MERCER MAYER

To the children of Roxbury

This is my town.
This is where I live.

These are the people
in my town.
They live here, too.

This is our post office.
The mail comes in here.
I come here to mail letters.

This is our fire station.

The fire truck lives here.

Oo! Ee! Oo! go the sirens.

When there is a fire,
the firemen go to it.
They put the fire out.

This is our police station.
Police officers work here.

They keep our town safe.

This is our diner.

Sometimes we come
here for lunch. Yum!

This is our town hall.

Our mayor works here.

Sometimes we have parades in our town.

This is our library.

I come here to find
books to read.

During story hour,
the librarian reads to us.

But when story hour is over
we have to be quiet.

This is our movie theater.

I can buy my own ticket.

I like to get popcorn.

I am always extra careful.

This is our store.

Sometimes Mom and Dad
let me walk here by myself.

This is our school.
My friends and I
are in Miss Kitty's class.

School is fun!

This is our park.

We play football here.

This is our bakery.

It has the best cupcakes.

This is the office
of our town newspaper.
It is a busy place.

Look! Last week
my picture was
in the newspaper.

This is my town.
It is the nicest place
in the whole world.